ADVENTURES of the
Steampunk
Pirates

Attack
of the Giant
Sea Spiders

Gareth P. Jones

Stripes

WANTED

DEAD OR ALIVE!
(or smashed into little bits and delivered in boxes)

The crew of the *Leaky Battery* the STEAMPUNK PIRATES for piracy, looting and treason.

Sixteen scurrilous scallywags in total, including their four officers:

CAPTAIN CLOCKHEART
Hot-headed leader of the Steampunk Pirates. He is unpredictable and dangerous on account of a loose valve sending too much steam to his head.

FIRST MATE MAINSPRING
Operated by clockwork, he is at his most dangerous when overly wound up.

QUARTERMASTER LEXI
Fitted with a catalogue of information, he is the cleverest (if not the bravest) of the bunch.

MR GADGE
His various arm attachments include all kinds of devilish weaponry and fighting equipment.

A REWARD OF
TWO THOUSAND POUNDS
is offered for anyone who captures this crew of loathsome looters and returns them to their rightful owner, the King of England.

We are the Steampunk Pirates,
We're ready for the fight,
We'll fight you in the morning,
We'll fight you through the night,
With rusting metal bodies,
Some say we're quite a sight,
Though gold's our goal,
We do need coal,
To keep our fires alight,
(Alight!)
To keep our fires alight!

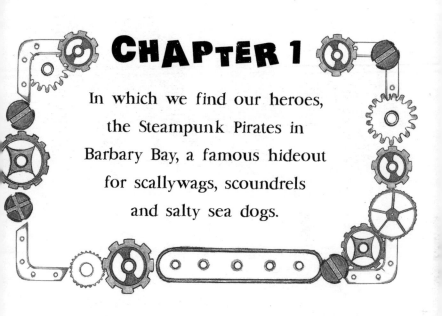

CHAPTER 1

In which we find our heroes,
the Steampunk Pirates in
Barbary Bay, a famous hideout
for scallywags, scoundrels
and salty sea dogs.

Of all the alehouses in Barbary Bay, The Slurring Mariner was the most dangerous, dirty and downright disgusting. Mrs Smellgrove's ale was strong, dark and served with a dead rat floating in it.[1] Her rock-hard pies had more chance of escaping unharmed than the customers who dared eat them.

---

1 A live rat was available for an extra penny.

But the four metallic men who stood at the bar had no interest in beer or food.

"Four tankards of your crudest oil, if you'd be so kind, landlady," said Captain Clockheart.

"Just water for me, actually," said Quartermaster Lexi.

Some landladies would have been confused by this unusual order, but Mrs Smellgrove simply poured out the three tankards of unrefined oil and one

glass of extremely murky-looking water. Quartermaster Lexi paid her and the Steampunk Pirates took their drinks.

"What brings you here to Barbary Bay tonight then, gents?" she asked.

"**Click**, to trade. **Tick**, looted goods. **Tock**, for gold," said First Mate Mainspring.

Captain Clockheart downed his oil and slammed the empty tankard back on the bar. The clock in the middle of his chest ticked loudly and steam gushed from his ears.

"Trading goods, eh?" said Mrs Smellgrove.

"Yes," Captain Clockheart replied. "We picked up some valuable items on our last few raids. We're here to exchange them for gold and coal."

"Why gold and coal?" asked the landlady, mopping up some dribbles of oil with a grubby cloth.

"We want gold to replace our rusting iron parts." The word-wheel in Quartermaster Lexi's head spun round as he spoke. "Coal is fuel, energy ... food."

"Aye, lassie. Gold for our parts, coal for our hearts," agreed Gadge.

"**Click**, not all of us care for coal," said Mainspring. "**Tick**, I run on clockwork."

"Don't we know it, you overgrown pocket watch!" said Gadge.

10

"**Tock**, what did you call me?"

Mainspring was reaching for his cutlass when the whole alehouse fell silent. A black-bearded man entered. He wore a large three-cornered hat with two small holes cut into the material, as though he had a pair of eyes on top of his head.

He glanced around the bar, brandished his cutlass and shouted, "Good news, you washed-up sea dogs! Old Inkybeard and Nancy are recruiting again. If you want adventure and riches, step forward now and join us."

"Join you?" shouted one drinker. "I heard you set fire to your last ship."

"It wasn't even yours to sink," said another.

"And your crew was still on board when it went down," said a third man.

"Now, Nancy, don't listen to the nasty men." The pirate removed his hat to reveal a squid sitting on his head, with its tentacles wrapped around his neck and shoulders.

"For those of you who are unfamiliar with my wife, this is Nancy."

The squid blinked.

"Evening, Inkybeard," said Mrs Smellgrove. "A bowl of mussels for Nancy, is it?"

"That'd be smashing, Mrs Smellgrove," he replied. "But it's the Dread Captain Inkybeard, if you don't mind."

"Oh yes, of course. Sorry," said Mrs Smellgrove.

"Hey, laddie, why have you got a squid on your head?" asked Gadge.

Inkybeard caressed a tentacle draped over his right shoulder. "Old Nancy's black ink helps keep my beard from going grey, don't it, girl? Now, we don't need to ask who *you* are. The ocean is awash with rumours of you metallic marauders. What will they think of next, Nancy?" Inkybeard walked around the Steampunk Pirates, inspecting

them carefully. He reached out to touch the spinning wheel on Lexi's head. "What's this for, then?"

"My word-wheel allows me to access information," replied Lexi. The wheel spun round and Inkybeard quickly withdrew his finger. "The Dread Captain Inkybeard," said Lexi. "Wanted in twelve countries for various crimes, including piracy, pillaging and stealing salmon."

"Nancy is partial to a bit of salmon, aren't you, girl?" said Inkybeard, stroking the squid.

"Inkybeard also has a reputation for betraying his crew and sinking his own ships," continued Lexi.

"You don't want to believe everything you read. So you're the brains – there's no need to ask who's the brawn." With the tip of his

cutlass, Inkybeard lifted up Gadge's barrel-like forearm and inspected it. It twisted around and a dagger attachment sprung out. Inkybeard moved away and turned his attention to the key slowly revolving in First Mate Mainspring's back. "What happens if I wind this up, then?" he asked.

"**Click**, give it a try. **Tick**, and find out," said Mainspring.

Captain Clockheart stepped in front of Inkybeard, steam shooting from his head. "I'm the captain and you'll leave my officers alone, if you know what's good for you."

"It's one thing to *call* yourself a captain. It's another to *be* one." Inkybeard waved away the steam gushing from Clockheart's head and turned back to the others. "If you lot have any sense, you'll get rid of this

bucket of steam and find a real captain for your vessel. As luck would have it, Nancy and I are currently in need of a ship."

"You won't set foot on the *Leaky Battery* while I have fire in my belly," said Captain Clockheart.

"And what if someone was to put out that fire?" threatened Inkybeard.

"**Click**, if anything happened to him. **Tick**, we'd replace him with one of our own," said Mainspring. "**Tock**, not a soft skin like you."

Inkybeard smiled at First Mate Mainspring. "Ah, is that ambition we detect? Nancy and I like a bit of healthy ambition."

"I suggest you walk away now." Captain Clockheart drew his cutlass and his clock hand whizzed round and round.

Mrs Smellgrove had seen enough fights

break out in her alehouse over the years to know the signs. She threw the filthy dishcloth over the pile of pork pies and took cover behind the bar.

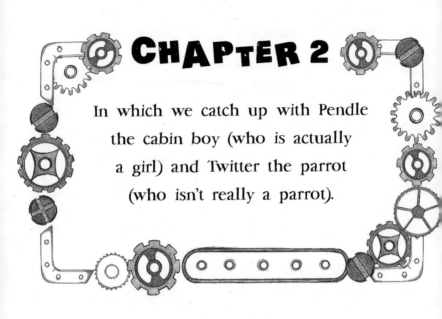

CHAPTER 2

In which we catch up with Pendle the cabin boy (who is actually a girl) and Twitter the parrot (who isn't really a parrot).

The *Leaky Battery* was tied to a rotten old signpost at the end of Barbary Bay's pier.

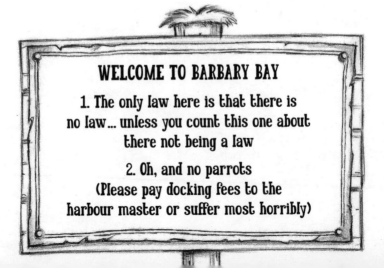

WELCOME TO BARBARY BAY

1. The only law here is that there is no law... unless you count this one about there not being a law

2. Oh, and no parrots
(Please pay docking fees to the harbour master or suffer most horribly)

The Steampunk Pirates' ship was not the only vessel tied to the rickety pier, but it was the only one that boasted a steam-powered engine at its heart.

Pendle the cabin boy paced up and down the pier. She was listening to the sounds from the mainland and trying to pick out the captain's voice in the hubbub.

Twitter fluttered down and landed on the railing in front of her.

"Something to eat! Something to eat!" squawked the mechanical bird.

"Hello, Twitter." Pendle held out a broom handle for the bird to nibble. "It's rosewood, your favourite."

Twitter pecked happily at the end of the broom handle and Pendle stroked the feathers glued to his metal body.

Pendle had created the steam-powered bird back when she was still known as Penelope Fussington and Twitter had always had a thing for rosewood.[2]

Twitter swallowed a couple of splinters then hopped along the rail. "No parrots!" he said. "No parrots allowed here!"

"I know. It's not fair, is it?" said Pendle. "Parrots aren't allowed and yet the most dangerous pirates in the world are. They're all armed with swords, cutlasses and pistols and, so long as they pay the harbour master for docking, they can do whatever they

---

2 If you'd like to know more about Pendle creating Twitter, the author politely suggests you pick up a copy of *The Leaky Battery Sets Sail*, the first of the Steampunk Pirates' adventures.

want. I don't like it."

The harbour master's house stood at the other end of the pier. Heavy iron chains hung below a balcony, holding an open treasure chest where visiting pirates placed their docking fees. It was always overflowing with stolen goods and glistening treasure.

"Where's everyone else?" asked Twitter.

"They're down in the hold," said Pendle. "Old Tinder is serving up a batch of charcoal. I'm keeping lookout while Blower grabs something to eat."

Pendle looked for approaching metal in among the constant stream of ragged pirates arriving and departing. She couldn't help but worry about Captain Clockheart. He was more than capable of looking after himself, but he didn't always think things through

properly. The loose valve sending steam to his head made him hot-tempered and unpredictable.

"I wish the captain would hurry up!" Pendle sighed.

"Back soon!" squawked Twitter. "He'll be back soon!"

"I hope you're right," said Pendle. "I'll be glad when we can leave this place."

Twitter flapped his wings and went soaring up into the evening sky.

"I only hope the captain's not getting into trouble," Pendle said to herself.

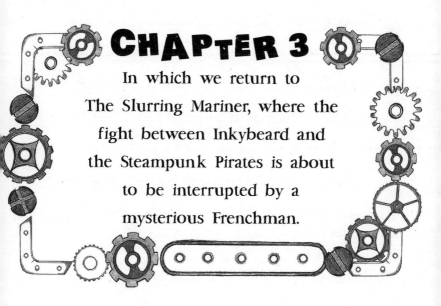

CHAPTER 3

In which we return to
The Slurring Mariner, where the
fight between Inkybeard and
the Steampunk Pirates is about
to be interrupted by a
mysterious Frenchman.

As with most fights that broke out in The
Slurring Mariner, every hard-knuckled
hooligan in the alehouse dropped what they
were doing and joined in. Within seconds,
three men had jumped on to Gadge's back.
He switched his arm attachment to a hook
and pulled them off one by one before

flinging them across the bar.

First Mate Mainspring used his cutlass to fend off a bare-chested man who smelled of beer, fish and feet. The man was strong but every single one of Mainspring's fight moves was executed with perfect timing.

On the other side of the room, Lexi took cover under a table next to a stranger with a long ginger beard.

"Excuse me," Lexi said. "Would you mind if I shared your hiding spot?"

"Not at all," replied the stranger, clinging on to his beard, almost as though he was worried it might get yanked off.

Captain Clockheart was locked in battle with Inkybeard. The steam-powered pirate swung his curved blade, but Inkybeard blocked it.

"Nancy and I will teach you a thing or two about being a real pirate." Inkybeard swished his cutlass then lunged.

Captain Clockheart parried and leaped on to a chair, which collapsed beneath his weight immediately.

"Mind my furniture, will you? Wood don't grow on trees," yelled Mrs Smellgrove. She threw a pork pie, which bounced off the back of Clockheart's head.

Fists, daggers and insults were flying all over the place when a tall man in a blue velvet jacket entered the bar. He had a thin moustache under his pointed nose and held a pistol in his hand. He climbed up on to a table, raised the pistol and fired at the ceiling. The old chandelier came crashing to the ground, sending glass everywhere.

Silence followed.

"Good evening, ladies and gentlemen. My name is Count Defoe." The man spoke with an accent as strong and French as the batch of smelly cheese that Mrs Smellgrove brought out whenever she wanted to clear the bar. "I am looking for recruits," he said. "Ambitious men, strong men and, most of all, men who want to be rich." He pulled out a cloth bag, tossed it into the air then fired at it. The bag split, sending coins raining down, and everyone scrabbled to collect the money.

"That's not fair," grumbled Inkybeard. "He can't just nab our recruits! We be here first."

"I am offering an opportunity of wealth," answered Count Defoe. "You only offer ze chance of betrayal." His gaze fell upon the Steampunk Pirates. "Ah, ze buccaneers of

metal, you are most welcome to join us."

"**Click**, no thanks," said First Mate Mainspring. "**Tick**, we don't work for soft skins. **Tock**, no more."

Count Defoe waved his hand dismissively. "Ah well. Now, ze rest of you, come with me to a land of opportunity."

He climbed down from the table and left, followed by almost everyone else.

"What about my chandelier?" yelled Mrs Smellgrove, emerging from behind the bar. "What about my customers?"

The reply came in the form of a small bag of coins, tossed back into the bar. She picked it up, counted its contents and went off to find a broom.

The author apologizes for this interruption, but he would like to draw the reader's attention to a scene that occurred two weeks earlier in London, England.

The King of England had called the Iron Duke and Admiral Fussington for a private meeting. Of the three men standing in the royal chamber, it was difficult to say who was the angriest. The king was angry with the Iron Duke. The duke was angry with Admiral Fussington. The admiral was angry

that he didn't have anyone to be angry with.

"Four ships!" exclaimed the king, turning the same shade of purple as the curtains. "Four ships at the bottom of the ocean and where are these metal servants of mine?"

"Actually, it was five ships," said Admiral Fussington. "They sank four ships when we first trapped them, then another when we trapped them a second time."

"Trapped?" screamed the king. "*Trapped?* Do you even know what the word 'trapped' means?"

The duke glared at Admiral Fussington.

"And it isn't just the ships, either," continued the king. "You lost weapons, expensive equipment and men. Do you have any idea how much your failure has cost so far?"

"I could make a rough guess, if you like?" suggested the admiral.

"Do not make a guess," said the Iron Duke firmly.

"These steampunk servants of Mr Swift's have turned out to be the worst birthday present since my father gave me a unicorn," said the king.

"A unicorn?" said Admiral Fussington. "That sounds like a wonderful present."

"It would have been – but it turned out to be a horse with a broom handle glued to its head."

"Your Majesty," said the Iron Duke, "I have a plan that will bring the Steampunk Pirates to justice. It involves Admiral Fussington, this large ginger beard and a place called Barbary Bay. You see—"

"Enough." The king snatched the false beard from the duke and threw it across the room. "Right now we have more pressing problems. That French scoundrel, Commander Didier Le Bone, is on the move."

"Ha," snorted the duke. "If there's going to be a war with France, then I will defeat Le Bone just as I defeated him before."

"Of course there's going to be a war," snapped the king. "We have one arranged for next June. Then we've got a couple of skirmishes with Spain pencilled in for the following autumn."

33

"Really?" said Admiral Fussington.

"Oh yes," the king explained. "Regular wars are good for a country – they keep everyone's spirits up. The question is not whether there *will* be a war, but whether the French will play fair. My spies tell me that Le Bone is making secret preparations in a remote American colony. His second in command, Count Defoe, is recruiting men, but the spies have no idea why."

"Do you think he's building an army?" asked the Iron Duke.

"That's what I need you to find out." The king led the duke and the admiral over to a large map and pointed out a part that had been coloured in with the red, white and blue stripes of the French flag. "There has been constant traffic along this coastline, but

we don't know where the ships are going. It's as though they're disappearing into an invisible cave."

"I see," said the duke. "And you want us to attack this cave?"

"You'll do no such thing. Haven't you been listening to a word I've been saying? If you go barging in, you'll end up starting the war early and we're not ready!"

"The Iron Duke was born ready," said the duke, puffing out his chest.

"I don't care about you," replied the king. "The European Royal Golf Championships are coming up and I think I stand a chance of winning. I've been practising my swing all year." The king demonstrated and accidentally whacked Admiral Fussington on the nose. "A war would completely ruin it."

"So what do you want us to do?" asked the admiral, holding his throbbing nose.

"I want you to conduct a secret mission … in secret. Find out where these ships are going and what that swine Le Bone is up to – without starting a war. Have you got that?"

"Yes, Your Majesty," said the duke. "I know a way we can discover the information and still capture those Steampunk Pirates. You see, my plan involves Admiral Fussington, this large ginger beard and—"

"I'm not interested in the hows and whys," interrupted the king. "Just get on with it."

The author hopes you found this scene informative and entertaining, but he now suggests returning to the story in hand.

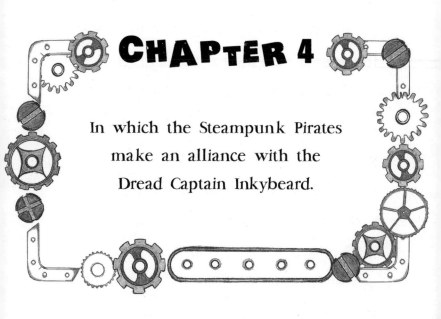

CHAPTER 4

In which the Steampunk Pirates
make an alliance with the
Dread Captain Inkybeard.

Back in the now-empty tavern, Inkybeard
picked up a glass of water and threw it over
the squid on his head. "There you go, Nancy
my love. Is that better?"

"There's no one to protect you now,
Inkybeard." Gadge twisted his arm and
produced an iron fist.

Captain Clockheart and First Mate Mainspring approached, threateningly.

"Now come on, lads," said Inkybeard, with an uncertain smile. "We're all on the same side. I don't know who Defoe thinks he is, flashing his cash and coaxing all those men to work for him, doing who knows what… He's the real enemy – not me."

"They never return, either," said the stranger with the ginger beard, climbing out from under the table.

"What was that?" asked Captain Clockheart.

"These men who go with Count Defoe – they never come back." The stranger scratched his chin as though his beard was bothering him. "I work for the, er … the harbour master here in Barbary Bay."

Gadge leaned in to take a closer look.
"I say, laddie, you look familiar."

The man backed away, clutching his
beard. "People do say I've got one of those
faces." He laughed nervously. "But the
point is that my boss, the, er … the harbour
master, is worried about this Defoe chap
recruiting all those men."

"Why?" asked Lexi.

"Isn't it obvious? The fewer pirates in the sea, the less money the harbour master makes. That's why he's offering a reward for information."

"What kind of reward?" asked Gadge.

"Gold, of course," said the stranger. "My boss is a wealthy man. If you want to get your hands on some of his gold, then you should find out where that Frenchman is taking all those men." He walked quickly across the room, then paused in the doorway. "Once you've discovered where they're going, come to the harbour master's house to collect your reward."

The door swung shut behind him.

"There is definitely something familiar about that man," said Gadge.

"These lily-livered soft-skins all look the same to me," said Captain Clockheart. "But if there's gold to be won then this be a mission for us."

"How can we can follow Defoe's ship without being seen?" asked Quartermaster Lexi.

"Nancy and I can help you with that," said Inkybeard. "You see, we already know where that ship is going."

"**Click**, how do you know?" asked Mainspring. "**Tick**, and why should we believe you?"

"I'll tell you," said Inkybeard. "It were one of those grey mornings when you can barely tell the sea from the sky. The only colour at all was the burning red of me poor old ship that had accidently caught fire after a nasty

case of mutiny. Nancy and me were doing a spot of fishing when we saw one of Defoe's unmarked ships. We saw where it went, too… Into a hidden cave. Give me command of your ship and I'll take you there. How about it?"

"No one commands the *Leaky Battery* but me," said Clockheart. "But since you need a ship and we need directions, you can join us as navigator in return for a fair share of the reward."

"Now, Captain, I have to question whether this is a good idea," said Lexi.

"Aye, old wheelie-noggin has a point," said Gadge. "Do we really want a rapscallion like Inkybeard on board the *Leaky Battery*?"

"While I'm the captain, I'll make the decisions," said Captain Clockheart.

"**Click**, *while* you are. **Tick**, you will," muttered First Mate Mainspring.

Captain Clockheart ignored him. "What do you say, Inkybeard?"

"We accept the terms!" he replied.

The two captains shook on the deal, but Clockheart held on to Inkybeard's hand, drew him close and whispered in his ear. "If I even get so much as a whiff of treachery, I'll send you and your squid on a short walk that ends with a big splash, if you get my meaning."

CHAPTER 5

In which Inkybeard boards
the *Leaky Battery*, meets Pendle
and discusses what makes
a good pirate.

"Yo ho, down below! The officers are
returning!" shouted Blower from the crow's
nest of the *Leaky Battery*.

"The captain's back!" squawked Twitter,
flying around excitedly. "The captain's back
and he's brought seafood!"

Loose-screw and Blind Bob Bolt lowered

the boarding plank while the rest of the crew gathered on the main deck. Captain Clockheart, his officers and Inkybeard stepped on board.

"Aye aye, Captain." Pendle saluted.

"Ah, Pendle lad, this be Inkybeard," Captain Clockheart said. "He'll be with us for the next few days."

"It's the Dread Captain Inkybeard, actually," said the black-bearded pirate.

"Not while you're on board my ship, it isn't," said Captain Clockheart. "I'm the only captain here."

"**Click**, for the time being," muttered First Mate Mainspring. "**Tick**, it'll be Captain Mainspring. **Tock**, one day soon."

"Now, First Mate Mainspring, don't force me to make an example of you again,"

warned Captain Clockheart. "Pendle, Inkybeard will require somewhere to sleep and something to eat."

"Don't worry about Nancy and me." Inkybeard pulled a small stick from his belt, which extended into a fishing rod. "We'll sleep under the stars and catch our own food. Nancy is very particular about her dinner, aren't you, my love?" He patted one of the squid's tentacles tenderly.

"Captain," Pendle spoke out of the corner of her mouth, "are you sure he's all right in the head, this fellow?"

"As loopy as a figure-of-eight knot, so he is," replied the captain quietly. "But he's got knowledge we need and he'll help us so long as he's helping himself. Still, I don't trust the scallywag, so keep your eye on him."

"You know it's rude to whisper," said Inkybeard.

Captain Clockheart looked up and said, "I was just telling my cabin boy not to treat you like a mere passenger, but more like a … what's the word now?"

Lexi's word-wheel clicked into action. "Friend? Chum? Pal?" he suggested.

"*Enemy*," said Captain Clockheart. "Now, Pendle, give Inkybeard a quick tour while

we prepare the ship. First Mate Mainspring, Gadge, Washer Williams, Tin-pot Paddy and the rest of you dented buccaneers, let's get this ship ready to sail."

Mainspring cried, "**Click**, you hear that, you lazy bunch of marauding meat forks. **Tick**, untether the ship, up with the sails, clean out the cannons. **Tock**, and let's be away."

Inkybeard placed a hand on Pendle's shoulder and gave it a little squeeze. "And what would a human cabin boy be doing in amongst all this hardware?" he asked.

Pendle wriggled out of his grip. "This crew may not have blood or bones but they've got more heart than any man I know."

"You've got spirit, lad. Soon Nancy and I will have a ship of our own, and you'd be welcome to come and work for us."

"These pirates are my friends," said Pendle. "You'll never find a more loyal, hard-working and honest bunch on the whole of the seven seas."

Inkybeard watched the crew as they climbed the rigging, swabbed the decks and performed all of the duties that so often caused human pirates to grumble and moan.

"Loyal, hardworking and honest, yes," he admitted. "But those aren't the things we look for when we're finding crew. It's qualities like bloodthirsty, fearless and dastardly that *we* want to see in a pirate."

"They can be all of those things, too – as you'll find out if you double-cross them," warned Pendle.

"Double-cross! Did you hear that, Nancy?" Inkybeard chuckled. "We wouldn't dream of

such a thing, would we?"

Inkybeard inspected the lever attached to the huge cogs in the middle of the ship. "What's all this, then?"

"It's a steam engine. It gives us extra speed when we need it. I designed it myself," explained Pendle.

"Impressive. There's more to you than meets the eye, boy," said Inkybeard with a knowing wink.

Pendle hurriedly tucked her hair into her hat and left Inkybeard to his fishing.

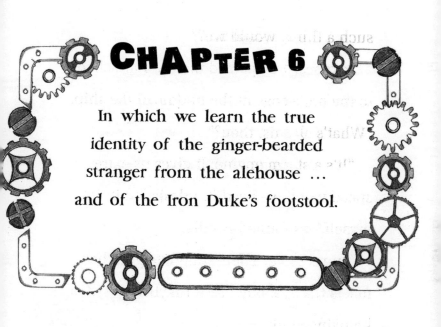

CHAPTER 6

In which we learn the true
identity of the ginger-bearded
stranger from the alehouse ...
and of the Iron Duke's footstool.

"Do you know, I rather like your view,
Harbour Master?" The Iron Duke leaned back
in his chair and rested his large black boots
on his footstool, which let out a soft moan.
He opened his book and had just started to
read when there was a knock at the door.

"Who is it?" he demanded.

"It's me, sir." The door opened and a man with a large ginger beard entered.

"Who are you and what do you want?" The duke stood up and drew his sword.

"It's me, Admiral Fussington." Fussington pulled off the false ginger beard as quickly as he could.

"Ah, Fussington, you fool. You're lucky I didn't run you through, taking me by surprise like that."

"Sorry, sir."

"How did you get on? Did you manage to trick Captain Clockheart into finding out what the French are up to?"

"Yes, sir. It went exactly as planned."

"Good. I just watched Count Defoe and his new recruits board the ship. The king is right – the French are definitely plotting something." The duke sat back down and put his feet up. His footstool groaned again. "I say. Who's that with the Steampunk Pirates?"

"His name is Inkybeard," said Fussington.

"Inkybeard?" The duke guffawed. "The Dread Captain Inkybeard? Even better.

He gets through ships like most men get through socks. Take a good look, Fussington. This may well be the last we see of the Steampunk Pirates."

"Wait a minute, I'm confused. Don't you want them to return with details of what Count Defoe and Commander Le Bone are doing? They can't do that if Inkybeard sinks their ship."

"As I see it, either they come back with the information the king wants and then we capture them, or they end up at the bottom of the ocean and we find someone else to do our spying. It's a win-win situation."

"But shouldn't we arrest them while they're here?"

"Arrest pirates in Barbary Bay?" scoffed the Iron Duke. "We'd have every salty

scallywag in the whole ocean on our backs, as my footstool would tell you."

"Your footstool?" The admiral noticed that the harbour master was down on the floor, tied up and gagged. The Iron Duke had been resting his feet on the harbour master, who was glaring angrily at the duke and trying to speak.

"When you're in Barbary Bay, you have to obey their laws, Fussington," said the Iron Duke.

"But Barbary Bay doesn't have any laws," said Admiral Fussington.

"It's got that one about parrots," said the duke. "I rather like that one."

"How can you abide by the laws of a place with no laws?"

"Any way you like," said the Iron Duke with a triumphant laugh. "Any way you like."

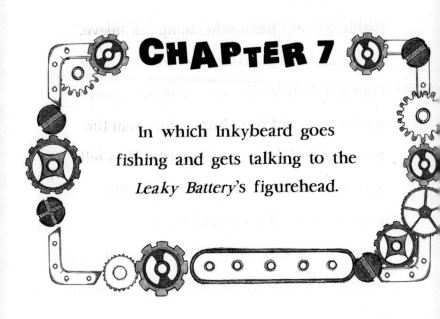

CHAPTER 7

In which Inkybeard goes
fishing and gets talking to the
Leaky Battery's figurehead.

For most of the journey, Inkybeard kept to
himself. When he wasn't giving directions,
he spent his time at the prow of the ship
with a fishing line dangling in the water.

"It won't be long now, Nancy my girl," he
muttered to the squid on his head. "Soon
we'll have a ship and crew of our own.

Old Inkybeard has a scheme up his sleeve."

Inkybeard was no stranger to one-sided conversations, so he was surprised when a reply came. Not from Nancy, but from the figurehead of the ship. "Hey, you! Do a fella a favour and catch me a fish, will you? I haven't eaten for a week."

Inkybeard leaned over the side of the ship and saw that the gold figurehead was talking to him.

"Hi," said the man. "Nice octopus hat."

"Don't say the 'o' word," whispered Inkybeard. "Me previous wife was an octopus and Nancy gets awful jealous, so she does. Are you another one of these steam-powered men?"

"No, no. I'm normal, like you. Well, I'm not married to a sea creature … but I'm human." The man spoke quickly and in a nasal American accent. "The Steampunk Pirates did this to me. They painted me gold and tied me to their ship. The name's Goldman, Chas Goldman. I'd shake your hand but, as you can see, I'm a little tied up."

Inkybeard chuckled. "Goldman by name and gold man by nature, eh?"

"I don't see what's so funny."

"What happened to you?" asked

Inkybeard. "Get on the wrong side of these machines, did you?"

Twitter landed on Goldman's head. "Tried to trick us!" he squawked. "Tried and failed!" The mechanical bird bit Goldman's nose then flew off again.

"I hate that bird," Goldman sighed. "Most of them have forgotten I'm even here, but that bird doesn't forget. He comes to taunt me every day."

"How've you survived?" asked Inkybeard.

"The cabin boy brings me fresh water when he remembers and, when the ship's moving, things get thrown up in the sea spray," he said, wincing in revulsion. "On a good day I'll catch a fish in my mouth."

"Raw fish. A man after Nancy's heart."

"Mostly it's seaweed."

Inkybeard guffawed. "You hear that, Nancy? We've got ourselves a gold-plated seaweed muncher."

"Don't you have any pity?" Goldman replied angrily.

"We ain't so big on pity, but I'll tell you what…" Inkybeard leaned further over so that he could speak quietly. "We'll get you off this ship if you help us when the time comes."

"I'll do anything to be free!" said Goldman.

"That's good to hear. Hold tight for now and, as a gesture of goodwill, we'll let you have the first catch of the day."

Inkybeard pulled on the line and lifted up a flapping fish. "Nancy, you don't mind if our new friend eats first, do you?"

Inkybeard swung the fish on the end of his line straight into Goldman's mouth.

"Thank you," Goldman said, biting down.

Inkybeard wrenched out the hook and dropped it back into the water. Nancy squeezed Inkybeard's head a little harder.

"Don't you worry, my love. The next one is all yours."

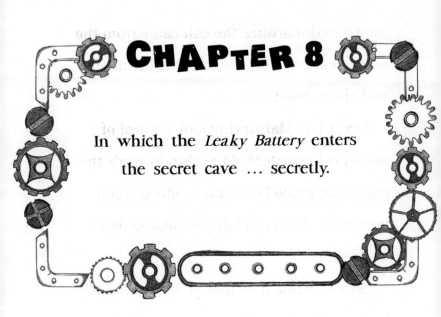

CHAPTER 8

In which the *Leaky Battery* enters
the secret cave ... secretly.

The *Leaky Battery* sailed for two days and
two nights without incident. Pendle kept a
close eye on Inkybeard the whole way. She
didn't like how much time he spent hanging
around the ship's engine, but she never
caught him doing anything wrong. The
wind was steady, the weather fair and, on

the second morning, the call came from the crow's nest, "Yo ho, down below! Land ahoy and cliffs ahead!"

First Mate Mainspring took control of the wheel and steered the ship towards the coastline, while Loosescrew and Wrench let out the jib to catch the wind and drive them in.

"Where's this invisible cave, then?" asked Captain Clockheart.

"If you could see it, it wouldn't be invisible," replied Inkybeard. "Maintain the current course."

A burst of scalding-hot steam erupted from Captain Clockheart's head. "Inkybeard, if this is a trick…"

"Oh, this is certainly a trick," he interrupted, "and a good one. But it's not

one I can take credit for. Now, lower the Jolly Roger. Only unmarked ships enter this cave."

"Lower the flag," ordered Captain Clockheart.

Pendle pulled on the rope and brought down the flapping skull and crossbones.

"**Click**, which way should I turn her?" asked First Mate Mainspring. "**Tick**, because if we stay on this course. **Tock**, we'll hit those rocks."

"Steady as she goes," said Inkybeard. "Ready the cannons."

Gadge spun round to face him. "All that squid ink has gone to your head, laddie, if you think we can blast our way through solid rock."

"We're not blasting our way through

anything," replied Inkybeard. "It's only the *sound* of cannon fire that we need."

"Captain, I strongly advise you to choose a different direction," said Quartermaster Lexi. "At this speed, the damage would be disastrous, catastrophic … fatal."

"We're all going to die!" added Twitter. "We're all going to die!"

"Light the fuses and fire the first cannon," shouted Inkybeard. "We'll need three in total."

"*I* give the commands around here," said Captain Clockheart. "You'd better be right about this, Inkybeard. Steampunk Pirates, fire the first cannon."

Washer Williams lit the fuse and the cannon flew back with the force of the blast. The cannonball shot harmlessly into the ocean and the sound echoed off the cliff.

"Two more shots like that," said Inkybeard.

"Two more of those," said the captain. "Mr Pumps, prepare the next cannon. Mr Hatchet, fetch more gunpowder."

"Can I ask the purpose of all this?" asked Gadge, over the boom of the cannon blasts.

"**Click**, Captain, **tick**, at this speed, **tock**, we're going to hit the rocks," warned Mainspring. "The *Leaky Battery* will be smashed to smithereens."

"I can't watch!" Lexi covered his eyes.

"Can't watch what?" asked Blind Bob Bolt, whose two eyepatches prevented him from seeing the huge cliff directly in front of them.

The cliff's huge shadow fell over the *Leaky Battery* and the crew prepared themselves for impact.

At the very last moment, the stone cliff moved.

There was a tremendous CREAK! as part of the cliff face slid to the side, allowing the ship to sail straight into the cave behind.

"Behold! The invisible cave," whispered Inkybeard.

"How interesting," said Lexi, uncovering his eyes. "Sliding doors disguised as a rock face. So this is how all those ships have managed to vanish without anyone seeing where they went."

"Aye," said Captain Clockheart, "but what lies on the other side that calls for such secrecy? That's what I want to know."

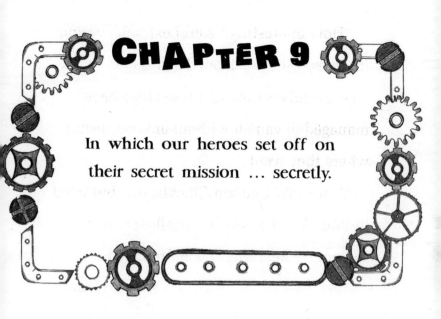

CHAPTER 9

In which our heroes set off on their secret mission ... secretly.

The *Leaky Battery* dropped its sails and the Steampunk Pirates rowed the ship into the cave. Inkybeard placed his hat over Nancy, being careful to line up the eyeholes so that the squid could see out.

"Sorry, girl. We'll need to keep you hidden for the time being." He turned to

Captain Clockheart. "The same goes for you lot. Lowering the flag ain't enough. If we're to convince them that we're one of Defoe's ships, you tin-can wonders had better get out of sight, too."

"Steampunk Pirates, below deck," ordered Captain Clockheart. The others followed the instruction but Clockheart remained. He grabbed two bits of cloth and wrapped them around his head and chin, then fastened his jacket to hide his metal body. Finally he pulled on a pair of leather gloves.

Inkybeard looked doubtfully at the vapour still gushing out of his head. "What about all the steam?" he said.

Captain Clockheart pulled out a pipe from his pocket and placed it in his mouth. "What steam?" he said. "This here be pipe smoke."

"Oh, *very* convincing," said Inkybeard doubtfully.

Inside the huge cave there were five more ships. All of them were tied to a wooden walkway built around the edge. A man in a blue uniform stood by the entrance, turning a wheel to operate the doors. Once they were shut, the man sighed, picked up a long stick of bread and took a bite.

"Dropping off or picking up?" he asked in an accent as thick and French as the baguette he was eating.

"Dropping off. We're bringing new recruits from Barbary Bay," said Inkybeard.

The man shrugged and said, "Dock your ship with ze others and continue on foot. *Au revoir*. Sorry, I mean goodbye. We're only to speak English 'ere. Not zat I 'ave anyone to talk to. Boring, stupid job... *And* my baguette is stale."

The man went into a small hut and Captain Clockheart brought the *Leaky Battery* in to dock between two much larger boats. The only light inside the cave was from oil lamps that hung off the walls.

Inkybeard gazed up at the other ships admiringly. "A nice collection of unguarded

vessels, eh, Nancy?"

"We're not here so you can steal a ship," said Captain Clockheart.

The other Steampunk Pirates reappeared.

"This is all a bit easy so far, if you ask me," said Gadge.

"Only because I knew the signal to get in," said Inkybeard. "Without us, you'd never have got so far."

"I'm not sure we should leave the ship here unguarded," said Lexi. "Perhaps I should stay behind."

"You'll come with me," said Captain Clockheart. "Mainspring, wrap yourself up, too. Gadge, you stay here and watch the ship with Pendle and the others."

"Why me?" said Gadge.

"Because something tells me we'll need

to be ready for a quick getaway," replied the captain. "And because it's hard to blend in with an arm the size of yours."

"Secret mission! Secret mission!" squawked Twitter.

"Hush up, you," scolded Captain Clockheart. "Twitter had better stay behind, too. He'll give us away as soon as he opens his beak. Pendle, make sure everyone keeps out of sight, will you, lad?"

"Aye aye, Captain," said Pendle. "Please be careful, Captain."

"Don't you worry, lad," said Captain Clockheart. "If I had a middle name, it would be 'Caution'. Now, where's that villain, Inkybeard?"

"He's there, leaning over the bow of the ship," said Lexi.

"Inkybeard, time to go."

Inkybeard turned round. He looked startled for a moment, then smiled. "All right, keep your springs on, we're coming."

Even with material covering the Steampunk Pirates' faces and bodies, they hardly looked normal. Pendle noticed that Lexi's word-wheel kept snagging on the scarf wrapped round his head and how strange Mainspring's key looked under the coat he was wearing.

"I've got a bad feeling about this, Gadge,"
she said.

"Aye, I know what you mean," said Gadge.
He cleared his throat and quietly sang a song
as the others disappeared down a tunnel.

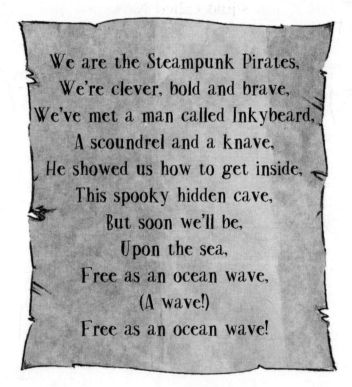

We are the Steampunk Pirates,
We're clever, bold and brave,
We've met a man called Inkybeard,
A scoundrel and a knave,
He showed us how to get inside,
This spooky hidden cave,
But soon we'll be,
Upon the sea,
Free as an ocean wave,
(A wave!)
Free as an ocean wave!

CHAPTER 10

In which we are offered a rare insight into the mind of a squid called Nancy.

It wasn't the first time Nancy the squid had been inside a cave, but this one felt different. Most of the smugglers' caves that she and Inkybeard visited were small and dark. This one went on and on, leading deeper and deeper underground. As well as the sound of dripping stalactites and

echoing footsteps, Nancy could hear the distant shouts of men, the cracking of whips and the clinking of metal against metal.

"It sounds as though there's some kind of workshop down here," said Quartermaster Lexi.

"**Click**, which would explain, **tick**, why they need, **tock**, all those men," said First Mate Mainspring.

"What are they making, though?" asked Captain Clockheart.

"Steady now, Nancy," said Inkybeard, feeling the tension in the squid's tentacles. "Everything is all right."

Of this, the only word Nancy understood was her own name. Not that it mattered what anyone said. So long as Inkybeard continued to feed and water her, Nancy would return

the favour with ink to keep his beard black.

It wasn't exactly the life Nancy had expected when she had been a baby squid, but if living on top of a pirate's head had taught her anything, it was that you never knew what was around the next corner.[3]

"Keep your voices down," said Captain Clockheart. "We're getting close."

An opening in the tunnel wall revealed a much larger cave, full of men hammering glowing bits of metal. The cave was hot and steaming from the great furnaces being used to heat the metal.

"It's an ironmonger's," said Inkybeard. "And a big one at that."

"It reminds me of somewhere," said Captain Clockheart.

---

3 For more insights into Nancy's thoughts, we recommend finding a copy of her autobiography: *Nancy: A Squid's Life as a Pirate's Wife*, although only a few copies were printed, due to lack of ink.

"**Click**, it's like Mr Richmond Swift's workshop," said Mainspring. "**Tick**, I was always our creator's favourite. **Tock**, until Clockheart came along."

Hundreds of men in ragged clothing were working away on the metal, with chains around their ankles. Soldiers in blue uniforms held whips and watched over them.

"So that's it. Defoe has got all these men working for him in this ironmonger's," said Inkybeard. "That French swine is turning good honest pirates into slaves."

"Can we go back to the ship now?" asked Lexi.

"**Click**, not until we know what they're making," said Mainspring. "**Tick**, and that's where we'll find out." He pointed to a sign above a doorway:

DANGER
CONSTRUCTION AREA

"Just look at all this delicious fuel," said Clockheart, pointing to the piles of coal being used to feed the furnaces.

"**Click**, don't even think about it," said Mainspring.

"First Mate Mainspring is right," said Lexi. "You know how you get when you eat too much coal. All that extra energy can make you a little, ahem … rash."

"Ah, but a couple of bricks won't do any harm," said Clockheart.

"**Tick**, no. **Tock**, come on," said Mainspring.

Nancy watched as the three pirates ventured into the workshop.

"This is where we say goodbye to our metal friends, my love," whispered Inkybeard, turning and walking back down the winding tunnel.

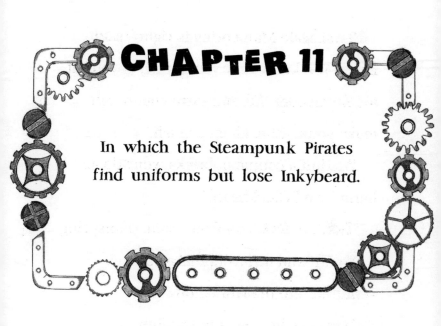

CHAPTER 11

In which the Steampunk Pirates
find uniforms but lose Inkybeard.

TINK... TINK... TINK...

The sound of iron being bashed into
shape filled the cave. All around, sparks
flew like exploding fireworks. Clockheart,
Mainspring and Lexi walked as casually as
possible through the workshop, unaware
that Inkybeard was no longer with them.

The pirates kept their heads down to avoid drawing any unwanted attention, but their disguises were falling apart.

"Captain," said Lexi, "I'm a bit concerned that these clothes are inadequate, poor … flimsy." As his word-wheel turned, the mechanism caught on the thread of his headscarf and unravelled it.

"**Click**, I agree," said First Mate Mainspring, whose key had worn through the coat on his back.

Captain Clockheart's disguise was no better. The steam blowing out of his head had made the material wet.

"Hey, you!" A blue-suited soldier pointed his pistol at them. "Where are you going and why are you not in uniform?"

"Leave this to me," said Lexi. "*Bonjour,*

84

mon ami. Je m'appelle…"

"No French," snapped the soldier.

"Sorry," said Lexi, "we've only just arrived."

"Zen you must go over zere where you will find uniforms." The man pointed at the far side of the workshop. "Ze boss will not be 'appy if he sees you in rags."

"He'll not be *a pea*?" said Clockheart.

"'*Appy*," said the soldier. "As in, if you are 'appy and you know it, clap your 'ands. Now, GO!"

"We'd better do as he says," whispered Lexi.

"Right." But Captain Clockheart wasn't listening. He'd spotted a trolley of coal trundling past. "Don't mind if I do." He reached up to snatch a lump, but First Mate Mainspring grabbed his wrist.

"**Click**, no," he said. "**Tick**, if anyone sees
you eating coal, **tock**, we'll all be exposed."

"What are you waiting for?" demanded
the soldier, eyeing them suspiciously.

"Nothing," said Captain Clockheart,
dropping the coal.

The pirates made their way to the other
side of the cave. As they passed one chained

man, they heard him sing a slow ballad to the rhythm of his banging hammer.

They promised me fortune
Treasure and wealth,
They said that the work would be
Good for me health,
But they tricked me and trapped me
And slapped on this chain,
And sometimes they beat me
And bring me great pain.

"Stop that. No singing allowed," yelled a soldier, cracking his whip.

In the corner of the workshop, the pirates found crates of blue uniforms piled high. "Fetch four, Lexi!" said Clockheart.

"Er, Captain, I think we only need three," said Lexi.

"What?" The captain spun around to find that Inkybeard had gone.

"**Click**, he must have given us the slip, **tick**, back at the entrance, **tock**, to the workshop," said Mainspring.

"Maybe it's not such a bad thing," said Lexi. "If you ask me, he's been trouble since the start."

"Aye, you may be right," said Captain Clockheart. "Let's get ourselves into uniform so we can find out what's going on here."

CHAPTER 12

In which Pendle visits the
dining cabin and experiences
the unfortunate side effects
of door handles.

There were three reasons Pendle didn't
usually join the crew at meal times:

1. She didn't eat coal (or charcoal or bits
of broken-up furniture), which is all that
Old Tinder the cook served.

2. Some of the greedier crew members
would sing very loudly and out of tune.

3. All that fuel produced some foul noises and smells from the crew.

But since there was little else to do inside the cave, Pendle sat down at the large oak table next to Gadge in the dining cabin of the *Leaky Battery*.

"Grub's up." Old Tinder wheeled himself in with a large steel pan on his lap.

"Let me give you a hand with that," said Gadge.

"I'm perfectly capable, thank you very much," said Old Tinder. He chucked the pan on to the table so that its contents spilled out.

"What is it today?" asked Loose-screw.

"A couple of tables, a sideboard and a cabinet," said Old Tinder. "I removed the glass, chopped up the wood and seasoned it with fish oil. Delicious, if I say so myself."

The pirates wasted no time in grabbing the bits of wood and chomping them down.

"Make yourself useful, Pendle lad," said Old Tinder. "Pour out the water. After all, we need fuel to burn, but it's steam that keeps our pistons pumping."

Pendle picked up a jug of water and walked round the table, filling everyone's cups.

"Thanks, laddie." Gadge downed the water then used his skewer attachment to pick up a piece of wood. "All this waiting around's no fun, is it?"

"It's awful," said Pendle. "I don't like this business at all. They're off with that Inkybeard and we're stuck inside this big cave. We should be out at sea being pirates, not spying for a harbour master that we've never even met."

"You know what the captain's like when he gets an idea in his head," said Gadge.

"And what if Mainspring decides to do something silly? You know he still wants to be Captain. Why can't he just accept that Clockheart is in charge?" Pendle went on.

"Search me," said Gadge.

"I'll tell you why," said Old Tinder.

"Because he thinks clockwork is better than steam power, that's why."

"Aye. He finds all this combusting disgusting," said Hatchet, letting out a loud gassy burp that smelled strongly of furniture polish. "Sorry, I think that was a door handle. Door handles never agree with me."

"Better out than in, eh?" said Gadge.

"I never really understood why Richmond Swift only made one of you clockwork," said Pendle.

"Swift was always tinkering with our design," said Old Tinder. "With each one of us he learned how to improve on the last one. I was the first one he made. Mainspring was supposed to be the last. *He* was supposed to be our leader."

"I've never heard about this," said Gadge.

"Oh yes." Old Tinder had got the whole room's attention. "Swift made him clockwork because he thought it would be more accurate … more reliable. Mainspring was his favourite. He used to tell him so, too."

"I remember that," said Blind Bob Bolt. "Then one day he came up with the idea for a steam-powered pirate with a clockwork heart. That was Clockheart, Swift's new favourite and our captain."

"Aye," said Old Tinder. "Mainspring never got over that."

None of this was making Pendle feel any better about Clockheart and Mainspring having disappeared down a tunnel together, but that wasn't the reason she made her excuses and left the dining room.

It seemed that door handles had an equally revolting effect on a number of the other crew members, too.

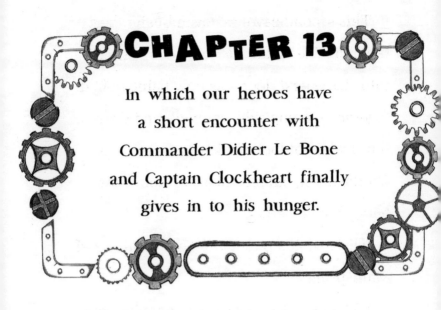

CHAPTER 13

In which our heroes have
a short encounter with
Commander Didier Le Bone
and Captain Clockheart finally
gives in to his hunger.

Dressed in their blue uniforms, Captain
Clockheart, First Mate Mainspring and
Quartermaster Lexi made their way across
the factory floor but, by the time they
reached the entrance to the construction
area, their clothes were already showing
signs of wear and tear.

This second cave was even busier than the first. The metal that had been bashed into shape next door was now being bolted together. On one side, chained men were building what looked like enormous legs. On the other, curved sheets of iron were being fixed together.

"**Click**, what are they making?" whispered Mainspring.

"Whatever it is, we've seen enough now," said Lexi. "Shouldn't we get back to the ship?"

"In a minute," said Captain Clockheart. "I want to know who that is."

In the centre of the room stood a man surrounded by armed guards. He wore a large hat, high heels and a jacket covered in so many medals that he had to lean back to

avoid falling forwards. Everything about the man's appearance was carefully designed to hide the fact that he was extremely short.

Lexi's word-wheel spun around. "Didier Le Bone," he said. "High commander of France and its armies."

"And there's Count Defoe," said Captain Clockheart.

The pirates approached the group quietly so they could listen in.

"As you can see," Defoe was saying, "our men are working around ze clock to meet your schedule."

"*Our* men?" said the tiny commander.

"Ahem." Defoe cleared his throat apologetically. "I mean, *your* men."

"Yes, *my* men," said Le Bone. "I am ze 'igh commander of all of France, ze leader of its armies, ruler of its people, and yet I am not 'appy. And when I am not 'appy no one else should be 'appy. You are working too slowly! 'Ow many Sea Spiders 'ave you made so far?"

"Only one. You see, our recruits are 'aving problems tightening ze bolts, but…"

"No more excuses. You are supposed to be creating ze weapons of ze future and yet

you 'ave made only one." Commander Le Bone kissed his fingertips in disgust. "Zese men are untrained, unskilled and unFrench! 'Ow do you expect to make progress with chained pirates doing all ze work? No wonder you are behind. You should make use of every able-bodied soldier."

"We are. Your soldiers are standing 'ere now because of your visit," replied Defoe.

"Is zat so?" Commander Le Bone spun on his heel and almost fell over. He regained his balance and turned to the nearest soldier. "You," he said. "Tell me, what 'ave you done to further ze cause of French world domination?"

"Me?" said the startled soldier. "Well, I've only been 'ere a short time."

"What did you say?" exclaimed

Commander Le Bone.

"A short time. A tiny bit," he continued. "A small—"

Suddenly Commander Le Bone let rip with an explosion of angry French words then he exclaimed in English, "I am Commander Didier Le Bone, ruler of France and soon to be ruler of ze entire world. I demand zat you all look up to me."

"You'd better stand on a chair, then!" shouted Captain Clockheart. "Or better still, a ladder."

Mainspring and Lexi turned to look at their captain and saw that his hands and mouth were stained black. He burped out a small cloud of coal dust.

Others were staring, too. Every soldier turned to look at him. In his fists, Captain

Clockheart held two large bricks of coal. He had finally given in to the temptation of all that delicious-looking fuel.

"Who is it zat dares to offend me, ze High Commander?" yelled Le Bone.

"High?" Captain Clockheart chuckled. "I've seen higher earthworms than you. I've seen taller ants. I've seen bigger shrimps."

"Captain." Lexi spoke out of the side of his mouth and tugged Clockheart's sleeve. "Remember what I said about eating too much coal?"

"Leave me alone," said the captain, pulling his arm free and taking another bite of coal. "I'm enjoying myself. What's the point of anything unless you enjoy yourself a bit!" He held up the lump of coal and gazed at it admiringly.

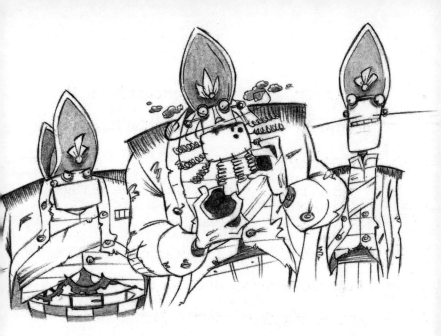

"Could someone explain why zis man is eating coal?" demanded Le Bone.

"**Click**, because he is a fool," said First Mate Mainspring pointedly. "**Tick**, and his engine is burning so hot he's not thinking straight... **Tock**, and he's going to get us all killed."

"Commander Le Bone," said Count Defoe. "May I present ze Steampunk Pirates! Guards – surround zem."

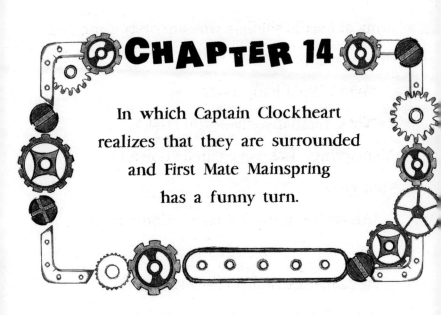

CHAPTER 14

In which Captain Clockheart
realizes that they are surrounded
and First Mate Mainspring
has a funny turn.

"**Click**, you and, **tick**, your stupid love of, **tock**, coal." Mainspring emphasized each word with a slap to Captain Clockheart's face.

Clockheart grabbed his first mate's hand to prevent him hitting him again and blinked. "What's going on?"

"We're in a secret cave, surrounded by an

army of hostile soldiers who are preventing our escape," said Lexi.

"Why? What happened?"

"**Click**, *you* happened," said First Mate Mainspring. "**Tick**, yet again let down by your greed."

"Ah, ze Steampunk Pirates." Count Defoe pushed his way through the soldiers with Commander Le Bone following behind. "So you decided to come and work for us after all. How nice. You even have uniforms, I see. How stylish you look."

"What intriguing machines," said Didier Le Bone, peering up at Clockheart's chest.

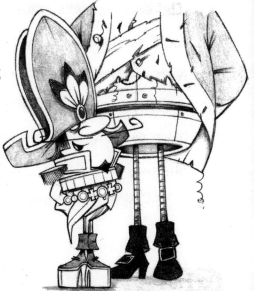

"Yes, you will be a welcome addition to my army."

"We work for no one." Captain Clockheart drew his cutlass.

Le Bone shrugged. "You would rather be destroyed? Very well. Zat can be arranged, too."

"A kind offer to be sure, but my officers and I will have to decline," said Captain Clockheart. The hand on his clock whizzed around.

"It's not an offer," said Le Bone. "It's a fact."

"Then let me tell you a fact," said Captain Clockheart. "In a moment you and your soldiers are going to step aside and watch helplessly as we walk out of this cave then make our getaway."

Le Bone and Count Defoe laughed.

"And why exactly would we do zat?" asked Defoe.

"Because too much coal might make me go a little crazy, but it's nothing compared to what happens when my first mate gets wound up."

Captain Clockheart handed his sword to First Mate Mainspring then grabbed the key on his back and twisted it round and round until it would turn no further.

"What are you waiting for, men? Permission from your mothers?" yelled Count Defoe. "Attack zem!"

The soldiers raised their swords and pistols, but Mainspring's arms were whizzing around like a pair of deadly windmills. Defoe's men backed off, clearly scared of being caught by the rotating blades.

"**Clickerty-tickerty-click**, that's it. **Clickerty-tickerty-tick**, step back. **Clickerty-tickerty-tock**, I'll mow you down." First Mate Mainspring spoke quickly as he cleared a path through the wall of soldiers.

"I will not be 'appy if you let zem escape!" cried Le Bone.

"Looks like you have to live with not being *a pea* then," said Captain Clockheart.

He and Lexi walked behind First Mate
Mainspring until they reached the doorway,
where they broke into a run.

"After zem!" yelled Le Bone. "All of you,
after *les pirates de Steampunk*."

The author apologizes for interrupting this exciting chase scene but he wonders if you might be interested in what Inkybeard has been doing since we last saw him.

As soon as Inkybeard saw all those strong men chained up and enslaved, he came up with a plan.

"If we're going to take one of them big ships, Nancy, we'll need a crew of about twenty men," he muttered, as he made his way back along the tunnel.

"Hey you. Who are you talking to?"
A large soldier standing in front of him
pointed a fat finger in Inkybeard's face.

"I'm talking to Nancy." Inkybeard took a
step back.

"Who's Nancy?"

"This is Nancy." He lifted his hat to reveal
the squid on his head.

The soldier gasped then received a face
full of black ink. Inkybeard whacked him
on the head and quickly stole his uniform.
Once he was dressed in blue, Inkybeard
continued along the tunnel until he came
across another soldier leading a bunch of
chained prisoners.

"Hey zere," Inkybeard said in a French
accent. "I'm supposed to take over from you.
You can 'ave a break."

"*Fantastique*," said the soldier. "I am starving. You'll need zese." He handed Inkybeard a key for the chain and a whip.

"Thanking you most kindly," said Inkybeard, with a bow.

He waited until the soldier had gone, then threw the keys to the prisoner at the front of the line. "Here, get out of those chains," he said. "You'll all be needing your hands soon enough."

"Wait a minute," said the prisoner. "You're not French. Who are you?"

"My name is the Dread Captain Inkybeard. Me and Nancy are here to rescue you."

"You hear that, lads?" said the prisoner. "We're free! Three cheers for the Dread Captain Inkybeard. Hip hip…"

"Hooray!" cheered the other prisoners.

Inkybeard silenced them with a crack of the whip. "You want to give us all away? Stay quiet until we get out of this stinking cave. Now come on, follow me."

The men were a rough selection of thugs

but Inkybeard wasn't worried. It was very rare that a crew betrayed him before he betrayed them. As he continued along the tunnel, he suddenly heard the sound of something clattering towards them.

"Quick, into this alcove. Someone's coming," Inkybeard said.

"We're not scared," said a prisoner with a crooked nose.

"Yeah, we'd welcome a good fight now we're out of those chains," said another with a face full of scars.

"There'll be plenty of time for fighting once we have a ship," said Inkybeard. "Now do as I say."

The men followed him into the dark corner. They had just managed to squeeze in when the three Steampunk Pirates charged

past, closely pursued by so many soldiers that it took several minutes for them all to pass.

"What was that?" asked another of the prisoners.

"That is what Nancy and I call a welcome distraction," said Inkybeard. "This day just keeps getting better. It's time to steal a ship."

Now let's get back to that exciting chase scene, shall we?

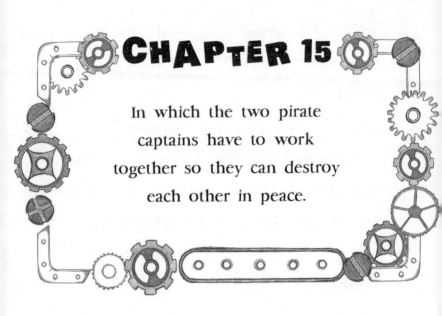

CHAPTER 15

In which the two pirate
captains have to work
together so they can destroy
each other in peace.

The Steampunk Pirates charged down the
tunnel with the French soldiers hot on their
heels. Clockheart and Mainspring were
having no problem running fast, but Lexi
was huffing and puffing and falling behind.

"I was not designed to move this fast,"
he grumbled, as his word-wheel spun. "I'm

unsuited, unqualified … ill-fitted."

"Unfit is what you are," replied Captain Clockheart. "Here, take a bite of this." He tossed a piece of coal over his head.

Lexi caught it and took a bite. As the fuel landed in his combustion engine, he felt a fresh burst of energy and caught up with Mainspring.

"**Clickerty-click**, this is all your fault, Clockheart. **Clickerty-tick**, if you hadn't given us away. **Clickerty-tock**, we wouldn't have half the French army after us."

"Now where would the fun be in that?" chuckled Captain Clockheart. They reached the tunnel's end and came out on the wooden walkway by the *Leaky Battery*.

"Yo ho, down below," yelled Blower with a shrill whistle. "The captain's returning."

"And he's got company," squawked Twitter.

"Mr Gadge, it's time for that quick getaway," shouted Captain Clockheart, as he hurried along the walkway.

"You heard the captain," cried Gadge. "Loose-screw and Rust Knuckles, untie the ship. Washer Williams and Blind Bob Bolt, to the cannons. The rest of you, get the oars – let's get this ship moving … QUICKLY!"

"Don't let zem escape!" Count Defoe shouted, as he and his soldiers emerged from the tunnel. "Anyone with sailing experience, man ze ships."

Captain Clockheart, Mainspring and Lexi leaped off the jetty and grabbed on to the ropes dangling over the side of the *Leaky Battery*. All three were hauled up on to the deck and the ship began to move.

In all the excitement, none of the French
soldiers noticed a black-bearded pirate and
twenty unchained prisoners sneak out behind
them and board one of the other ships.

"Inkybeard!" squawked Twitter. "Old squid-head's back!"

"Aye, and it looks like he's got the crew and ship he was after," said Pendle.

"Not for long," Captain Clockheart said. "Gadge, prepare the cannons. We'll make this the shortest journey of his life."

"Much as I'd love to blast that squid-loving loon out of the water, we have more pressing problems," responded Gadge. "We need to get out of this cave."

"We're all going to die!" squawked Twitter. "We're all going to die!"

"Ahoy there, Steampunk Pirates!" yelled Inkybeard from the bridge of his newly stolen ship. "Are you ready for lesson one? Always have a getaway plan."

"We have a plan," said Captain

Clockheart. "We'll ram these doors open and be away."

"The impact would smash your boat to pieces," shouted Inkybeard.

"He's right," said Gadge. "She simply couldn't take it, Captain."

"Don't worry. Leave this to old Inkybeard. Mr Goldman, the doors please."

"My pleasure, Dread Captain," replied the American. He was still covered in gold paint, but no longer tied to the front of the *Leaky Battery*. Instead he was standing at the end of the walkway. The guard who had let them in was nowhere to be seen. Goldman turned the wheel and opened the huge doors.

Three of Inkybeard's strongest men threw a rope around Goldman and dragged him

up on to their deck. With everyone on board
and the doors open, both ships rowed out of
the cave.

"This is all very well," said Lexi, "but what about Defoe's ships?"

Behind them Defoe's men were climbing on to the remaining ships, releasing them and preparing to fire the cannons.

"Blast all of zese pirates to pieces," Defoe yelled.

"We'll never survive such a—" Lexi was cut off suddenly when Captain Clockheart knocked him on the back of his head and shut him down.

"That's quite enough of that," he said. "Gadge, have you got anything that will cut through the rope that opens and closes the doors?"

"As it happens, I do." Gadge switched his arm attachment to a crossbow, pulled it back and fired. The arrow flew through

123

the air and sliced the rope cleanly. With the mechanism broken, the huge doors crashed shut, sealing off the cave and preventing Defoe's ships from following them.

There was a moment of calm as both ships floated next to each other in the open sea, then Inkybeard broke the silence. "Now we've got rid of that lot, it's time for your final lesson – the meaning of defeat."

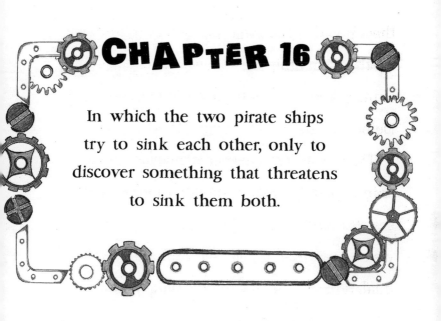

CHAPTER 16

In which the two pirate ships
try to sink each other, only to
discover something that threatens
to sink them both.

Nancy clung on tightly to Inkybeard's head
as the two ships fired their cannons. They
drew alongside each other and swung into
battle.

"Right, you liberated looters," yelled
Inkybeard. "You recently rescued ruffians.
Now it's time for you to repay your debt and

send these tiresome tin cans to the bottom of the deep blue sea."

Inkybeard's crew cheered and leaped on to the Steampunk Pirates' ship.

"For the *Leaky Battery*," yelled Captain Clockheart, who was defending himself against a thuggish pirate. The captain ducked, then lunged with his cutlass, sending his attacker staggering back.

First Mate Mainspring jumped on to the neighbouring ship and brought down his

blade on Inkybeard, who blocked the attack. The pair stood face to face. Cutlass to cutlass. Machine to man.

"You know you'll never be captain with Clockheart in your way," whispered Inkybeard. "Join us and we'll show you the true meaning of piracy."

"**Click**, never."

Mainspring's cutlass missed Inkybeard, but he caught him off guard with a kick to the chest. Inkybeard staggered back and Nancy slid down over his face, covering his eyes. He adjusted the squid then looked at Mainspring with newfound anger in his eyes.

"Now look what you've done. You've upset Nancy. You'll pay for that!" Inkybeard charged at Mainspring, who dodged out of the way. Inkybeard spun round and rammed his sword into Mainspring's back, preventing his key from turning.

"**Cuh-cuh-cuh**—"

The key rattled hopelessly against the sword and First Mate Mainspring ground to a halt.

"That's hardly fair now, laddie." Gadge landed on the deck in front of Inkybeard, aimed his gun barrel and fired.

Inkybeard dived out of the way, dropping his sword and releasing the key so that First Mate Mainspring came back to life.

"**Cuh-click**... Thanks."

All around, pirates were fighting. A large man with a hairy chest and ears like cauliflowers had Pendle up against the ship's engine. He knocked the dagger from her hand and approached menacingly. His blade glistened in the sunlight. Pendle was unarmed and there was no one to save her.

She closed her eyes and waited.

Nothing happened. She opened her eyes and saw the man looking up, his eyes wide with fear.

"W-w-what is that?" he stammered.

A dark shadow had fallen over them.

Pendle turned round. A huge mechanical contraption loomed over both ships. It looked like an enormous metal spider with legs that disappeared into the water. There were two eye-like windows in the spider's body. One by one, every battling buccaneer stopped to stare at the incredible sight.

Clouds of steam gushed out of a chimney on top and a pair of sharp pincers fired out hooks and wrapped ropes around each of the ships' main masts.

"Weigh the anchor," yelled Captain Clockheart, "or it'll snap off the mast."

"He's right," yelled Inkybeard. "Drop the anchor, lads."

Cannons dropped down from inside the spider's head and swivelled around, targeting the pirates. One of the spider's eyes opened and Commander Didier Le Bone stuck his head out of the window.

"Hah! You pirates are 'elpless against my Sea Spider. As you can see, unlike ze other ships it can travel underwater. Its legs are so long zey walk on ze bottom of ze ocean, and it has ze firepower of five warships."

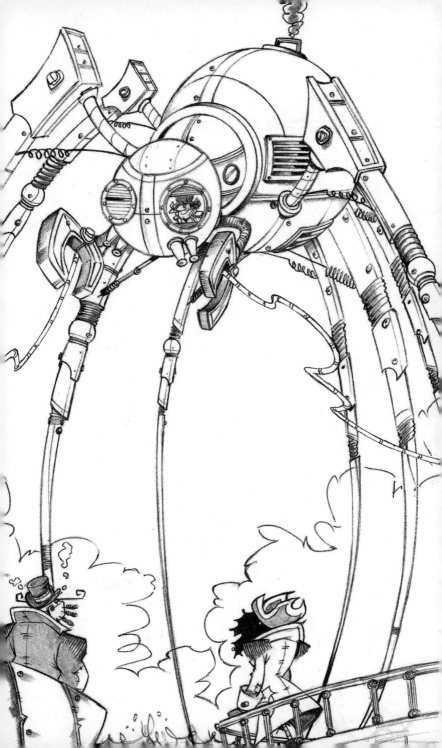

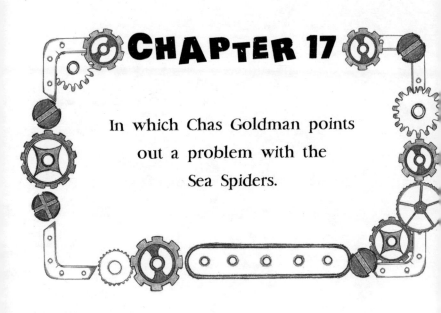

CHAPTER 17

In which Chas Goldman points
out a problem with the
Sea Spiders.

None of the pirates had ever seen anything

like the terrifying war machine that stood

before them. The Sea Spider had enough

firepower to sink them in an instant. With

its body raised high above the water's

surface, it towered over their wooden ships.

How could they sink something that was

already standing on the ocean's bed?

The Sea Spider bent its knees and brought Commander Le Bone level with the ships. He looked at the two captains with great interest.

"Ah, Inkybeard and ze famed Steampunk Pirates," said Commander Le Bone. "You will make ideal target practice for zis war weapon of the future."

"We'll fight to the bitter end," said Captain Clockheart.

"Yes, you will," said Le Bone.

"Don't shoot," yelled Chas Goldman, who was standing behind Inkybeard with his arms in the air. "I'm an innocent prisoner. By all means sink both these ships, but I beg you to spare my life."

"Goldman, you coward," snarled Inkybeard.

"Why should I spare you?" asked the French commander.

"I could be of use to you. I myself have some experience of steam engineering. I could help you improve these Sea Spiders."

"Improve? Pah, I do not need any 'elp," responded Le Bone. "I designed zis Sea Spider myself and it is perfect, as you will learn when we sink the lot of you."

"Really?" said Goldman, "because it looks to me as though the bolts in the leg joints are a little loose." He winked at Twitter, who was flying around his head.

"Loose bolts!" squawked the bird.

"Exactly," said Goldman. "Loose bolts."

"Nonsense!" replied Le Bone. "My design is flawless. Now we will deal with you pathetic pirates and get back to ze business

of taking over ze world!"

Twitter flew over to the Sea Spider and started pecking at its legs.

Captain Clockheart smiled. "There appears to be a little problem with that plan," he said.

"**Click**, an incy-wincy problem," said First Mate Mainspring.

"Aye, just a wee one," said Gadge.

"What? What? What? You dare to stand zere and make jokes about my size?" cried Le Bone.

"This is no joke." Captain Clockheart held out his arm and Twitter fluttered down and landed on his wrist. "Is it, Twitter?"

"Loose bolts!" cried the bird, dropping a pile of metal nuts into Clockheart's hand.

"What?" exclaimed Le Bone.

"How's the fishing today, Inkybeard?" asked Captain Clockheart. "Any Sea Spiders need throwing back into the sea?"

"Let's see." Inkybeard extended his fishing rod and prodded the head of the spider.

All it took was one push. There was a low moaning sound and the enormous spider tipped back. The few remaining bolts flew out and the spider hit the water, creating an enormous **SPLASH!**

The pirates cut through the ropes holding the masts and the ships drifted apart.

"You'll regret zis. I am a dangerous man to have as an enemy," yelled Le Bone. "This is not the last you'll—"

His words were cut off as the spider sank beneath the water's surface. Great waves rocked the ships as Le Bone's war machine vanished, followed by the eight detached legs.

"Well done, Twitter," said Captain Clockheart, patting the bird.

"We've got Goldman to thank, too," said Pendle.

"Och, I don't think he's hanging around for us to say thank you," said Gadge.

"What?" Captain Clockheart turned to see that Inkybeard's ship was already on the move. His crew had put up their sails and were now travelling away at great speed.

"**Click**, he means to collect the harbour master's reward," said Mainspring.

"Over my dead embers," yelled Captain Clockheart. "Pendle, fire up the engine. We'll catch up with that ship easily enough."

Pendle pulled on the lever to start the engine, but nothing happened. "Something's wrong," she said.

The engine made a strange gurgling noise then shot out a jet of black ink at Pendle's face.

"Squid ink," she said, wiping her eyes. "We've been sabotaged."

"Then we'll have to catch them the old-fashioned way," said Captain Clockheart. "Let's get some wind in these sails."

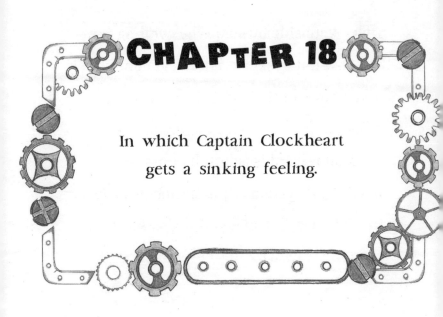

CHAPTER 18

In which Captain Clockheart
gets a sinking feeling.

The *Leaky Battery* chased Inkybeard's stolen
ship all day and all night. It took Pendle a
long time to rinse out all of the squid ink
from the ship's engine. Once it was clean,
she fired it up, which gave them enough
extra speed to catch up. By the time Barbary
Bay finally appeared on the horizon, the two

ships were side by side. The evening sun was low in the sky and both captains stood at the bows of their ships, glowering at each other.

"That reward is rightfully ours, Inkybeard!" yelled Captain Clockheart over the sound of the chugging engine and the crashing waves.

"The Dread Captain Inkybeard, if you don't mind!" he responded.

The ships cut through the water with full sails.

"Er, Captain, I fear that we're going to crash into the pier," warned Lexi.

"Rather that than lose to this scoundrel," replied Captain Clockheart.

"Full speed ahead!" yelled Inkybeard.

Both crews braced themselves. Even if the pier had been brand new, the damage from the ships hitting it at such a speed would have been severe. Being made of old rotten wood, both pirate ships tore through it. The welcome sign went spinning off into the water and the pier splintered and snapped as the ships finally dropped anchor and came to a halt.

Captain Clockheart and Inkybeard leaped down on to the dock, each desperate to reach the harbour master's house first. Inkybeard panted and held on to Nancy while Clockheart sent up puffs of smoke like a speeding locomotive. When they reached the harbour master's house, a figure stepped out on to the balcony, but he kept to the shadows.

"Ah, my pirate spies," he said. "What information do you have for me?"

"Defoe is slapping men in chains and using them to build weapons," blurted out Inkybeard.

"No ordinary weapons, neither," said Captain Clockheart. "Steam-powered war machines called Sea Spiders. They walk on the bottom of the ocean. Now, where's our reward?"

"All in good time. You have both proved very useful. His Majesty will be most grateful." The man stepped forward so that yellow lamplight fell on his face, illuminating his large bushy moustache and wicked eyes.

"It's the Iron Duke!" said Pendle, who was standing on the dock with the other Steampunk Pirates.

"What?" exclaimed Gadge. "You mean the duke was using us to spy for him this whole time?"

"**Click**, we've been tricked," added Mainspring.

"Duped by the duke!" squawked Twitter. "Duped by the duke!"

"Yes, yes, yes," said the Iron Duke with a dismissive wave of his hand. "You've been

working for me all along. Oh, what a shock. One–nil to me. The duke wins. Some good old-fashioned British planning has won over your sloppy piratical greed."

"You may have tricked us, but you can't touch us here in Barbary Bay," said Captain Clockheart.

"That's right," said Inkybeard. "Here, the only law is that there are no laws."

"And that one about parrots," said Lexi.

"No parrots!" squawked Twitter.

"Yes, I like that one," said the duke. "But, you see, with no laws there was nothing to stop me tying up the harbour master and assuming his identity. Isn't that right, Fussington?"

Admiral Fussington stepped on to the balcony behind the duke. "I suppose so,

although as a representative of His Majesty, the King of England—"

"Oh, stop talking," snapped the duke. "Anyway, I'm feeling generous, so you can have the reward. Fussington, let them have it."

"Very well, sir." Admiral Fussington unhooked the chains that held the large treasure chest, allowing it to drop suddenly. It smashed straight through the wooden walkway beneath and sent both Inkybeard and Captain Clockheart flying into the sea.

"Ha! You see, you've lost!" crowed the Iron Duke. "Goodbye, Captain Clockheart. Rust in peace. Do you get it, Fussington? *Rust* in peace?"

"Very good, Duke," said the admiral.

"No laws! No laws!" Twitter flew straight

up to the balcony and landed on the duke's shoulder.

"Get off me, you disgusting creature," he exclaimed.

"Fresh feathers! Fresh feathers!" Twitter fluttered around the duke's head, plucking red feathers out of his hat and sending them all over the place.

"Fussington, don't just stand there. Do something, man!" the duke protested.

"Yes, Duke." The admiral tried hopelessly to swat the mechanical bird away.

As he did so, a stray feather from the duke's hat went up Admiral Fussington's nose.

"A-a-chooo!"

The force of the admiral's sneeze sent him stumbling forward. He reached out for something to hold on to and grabbed the Iron Duke's moustache.

"Fussington, release me at—"

The Iron Duke and Admiral Fussington crashed into the balcony railing, which collapsed under their weight, sending both him and the admiral into the water.

Twitter performed a loop the loop then flew back to the balcony and into the harbour master's house, where he pecked through the ropes holding the harbour master captive.

In the water below, Inkybeard, the duke and Admiral Fussington swam to dry land. Captain Clockheart, however, had sunk like a stone.

"We have to rescue him!" yelled Pendle frantically.

"None of us can go underwater," said Gadge. "The seawater would put out our fires in a second."

"Then I'll go," said Pendle.

"You're not strong enough, laddie. You'd never lift him – you'd die trying."

"**Click**, *I* am strong enough. **Tick**, *I* have no fire to put out." Mainspring jumped on to one of the chains dangling down. "**Tock**, lower me in and make it quick. I've a captain to rescue."

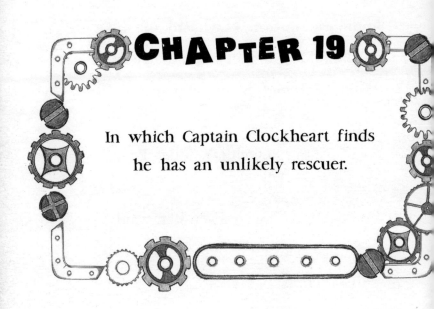

CHAPTER 19

In which Captain Clockheart finds
he has an unlikely rescuer.

Life at sea presented a number of problems
for the Steampunk Pirates. There was the
rust, the fact that metal does not float,
and the very real danger that if any one of
those steam-powered men were to fall into
the water, their fires would go out in an
instant.

But life at sea meant freedom and, for freedom, all that was a price worth paying. Captain Clockheart sank down into the murky depths of Barbary Bay. Water gushed into his body and rushed through his insides. It put out the fire in his belly and made him feel as light as a feather. He felt free.

As Captain Clockheart's fire was extinguished, the last thing to cross his mind was his earliest memory. It was the moment his creator, Mr Swift, had first lit his fire. Clockheart remembered opening his eyes and seeing his creator gazing at him with wonder and delight.

"Clockheart," said Mr Swift. "That's what you shall be known as. You are a steam-powered man with a clockwork heart – the best of both worlds. You will be the leader of these others."

Clockheart turned his head to see fifteen mechanical men staring back at him.

"They will follow your every order as you assist His Majesty the King."

"We will assist," Clockheart heard his own voice say. "We will assist."

This memory vanished as all of Captain Clockheart's thoughts were lost in the darkness and silence of the ocean bed.

"**Click**, dry him out. **Tick**, fetch fresh coal. **Tock**, relight his fire."

Clockheart was unsure where these words came from, but he knew who was speaking them. He felt the warm glow of life return and opened his eyes to see First Mate Mainspring leaning over him.

"**Click**, welcome back, Captain. **Tick**, it's good to see you."

"You could have let me drown," said Captain Clockheart groggily. "The ship would have been yours."

"**Click**, and give the duke the satisfaction of defeating you? **Tick**, not a chance. **Tock**, if anyone is going to get rid of you, it'll be me!"

"That's a comforting thought, Mainspring." Captain Clockheart sat upright.

"Captain, I thought I'd lost you." Pendle threw her arms around his neck.

"Let's not get sentimental now, lad," said

Captain Clockheart. "Where are the others? Where's Inkybeard?"

"We chased him off. He left with Goldman and that rough-looking crew of his," said Gadge. "They'll turn mutinous soon enough, I'll bet you."

"The duke and the admiral have also gone," said Lexi.

"Then it's just us and the ocean," said Captain Clockheart. "Exactly as it should be."

"But if we helped the duke get his information," said Lexi, "then this was all for nothing."

"Quartermaster Lexi, have you not learned? Adventure is never for nothing. Life at sea is about creating memories worth remembering. It's about living a life worth living," said Captain Clockheart. "Ain't that right, Pendle?"

"Aye, Captain. Besides, the harbour master has given us a reward for rescuing him."

Twitter flew down and landed on the captain's shoulder. "Back to the ship!" he squawked. "Back to the ship!"

"Aye, back to the *Leaky Battery*, ye marauding metallic mariners," cried Captain Clockheart. "I'll wager there's an ocean of adventure awaiting us just over that horizon."

When Captain Clockheart reached the *Leaky Battery*, the crew sang a raucously rousing sea shanty as they raised the anchor and set sail.

We are the Steampunk Pirates,
Your booty or your life,
We rob you with a cutlass,
And occasionally a knife,
We met a pirate captain,
Who caused some proper strife,
That Inkybeard,
Was awful weird,
With a squid that was his wife,
(His wife!)
Nancy was his wife!

OUT NOW!

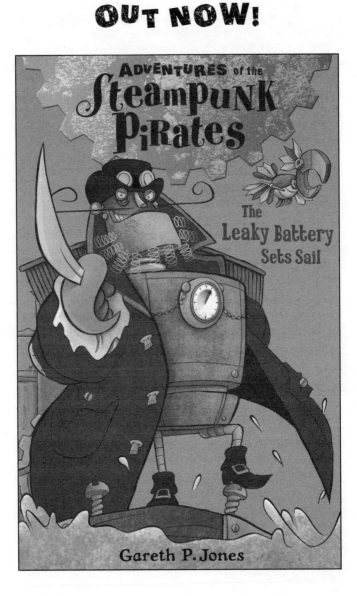

ADVENTURES of the
Steampunk Pirates

The Leaky Battery Sets Sail

Gareth P. Jones

COMING SOON!

Gareth P. Jones is the author of many books for children, including the *Ninja Meerkats* series, *Constable & Toop* and *The Considine Curse* (winner of the Blue Peter Book of the Year 2012).

When he isn't writing, Gareth can be found messing about in south-east London with his wife, Lisa, and their children, Herbie and Autumn. He spends an awful lot of time turning himself into a Steampunk Pirate. He has made a beard out of springs, a detachable clock heart and is currently learning how to play sea shanties on an accordion.

Find out more at:
www.garethwrites.co.uk